Long Walk Up

Childhood journey from tragedy to triumph

"However long the night, the dawn will

break."

African Proverb

"Long Walk Up breathes life into the resiliency of the African spirit. Through Turney, Mulukan easily leaves the pages and enters our hearts. You too will be encouraged to take the Long Walk Up."

Yaba A. Blay
Temple University Department of African American Studies

******

"Mulakan, child of Africa, orphaned without mother, father, and left without siblings, triumphs over the rocky terrain of her solo journey. Long Walk Up is a poignant story of survival."

Dr. Maxine Thompson, Butterfly Press

******

"Starting with her first book, Portia, and continuing with her latest effort, Long Walk Up, Denise Turney's literary expressiveness and dedication to the written word is evident. Long Walk Up is sure to be a bestseller."

Ron Kavanaugh, Mosaicbooks.com

"Anyone who trusts in him will never be put to shame." – Romans 10: 11

Long Walk Up
by Denise Turney
Copyright 2011

Scriptures are taken from the
New International Version of the
Bible. Copyright 1985,
Zondervan Corporation

Published by: Chistell Publishing

Cover: Morris Publishing

ISBN-13: 979-8812517472

Library of Congress Catalog Card Number: 2006931733

Contents

Dedication

For my son.

I love you, Gregory –

and for all those who have gathered courage, and who are, even now, walking up

Acknowledgements

Appreciation to the source of all eternal creations.

Thank you to my family. My father, Richard Turney. My mother, Doris Jean. My son, Gregory. My grandparents, Clyde and Emma Turney. My great-grandmother Rebecca Skinner. My brothers, Richard, Clark and Eric. My sister – Adrianne. My nephew and nieces, Richard, Angel, Assyria, Samaria, Megan, and John. My aunts, Christine and Pat. My uncle Donald. My great-aunt Ruby. My cousins Donna, Monica, Michael and Langston. Thank you for a foundation of love.

To my friends and supporters. To those who read, support and enjoy my books. To my church family, Norton Avenue First Baptist Church in Bristol, Pennsylvania where the Rev. James G. Evans III and his beautiful wife Sheila pastor. To my Sigma Gamma Rho sorors. To Tim and Essie Stackhouse, a woman who God used to allow the story of Ruth and Naomi to work itself into my own life. To Helen Crawford (I'll never forget you walking around the corner those many times just to see how I was doing). To Cormy L. Williams, one of the sweetest women I know. To Willie J. Murray – thank you for the sweet potato pies you made my son. To Mary Lambert, thank you for sound Sunday School lessons.

To <u>Long Walk Up</u>'s editor, Susan Bono – Thank you for sharing your skill and expertise. To everyone who has touched my life in a special way, thank you for your love and support.

Be courageous and take the Long Walk Up! --

Denise

Long Walk Up is a work of fiction. Although the book was read by peoples who have lived in Africa and although the author researched many facts about various customs and regions in the magnificent continent, particularly East Africa, the book is not based upon any single tribe or community within Africa, a place which may perhaps be the mother of all nations. Names to some places in the continent have been fictionalized. That said, the truths about the struggle, a child's destiny and the limitless power of love are real. And it is with the spirit concealed within these immeasurable truths that we bid you to begin the Long Walk Up.

Section I

Chapter One

Malaria, its feverish demands unrelenting, its grip firm, took more people from Guwati, Africa than starvation. The disease, settled into the region like maggots gone into dirt, and indiscriminately attacked toddlers, adults, newborns and elderly with nausea, diarrhea, painful swelling in the joints and inability to digest the scant food that remained on the windswept terrain. Three months had passed since a significant rainfall watered sorghum, maize and other major crops, and when rain did come, it seemed to only feed the malaria. The last of the healthy livestock, the noise of their pounding hooves going like log drums over the plain, the beat of their collective heart rushing toward escape, deserted the area weeks ago. Animals that hadn't moved were gaunt and fevered. Their bodies lay against the earth;

9

meat from their dehydrated limbs lingered as a gift to be consumed by the men, women and children after the meat was purged with fire.

Flames from the fire jumped and swayed the way the women did during Meskal, Ethiopia's two-day festival that had been celebrated for more than 1600 years. Meskal was a day that was filled with exploding colors, music, laughter, mouth-watering foods, and yellow daises bunched together then burned in commemoration of the discovery of the crucifix, the cross upon which Jesus was crucified, a discovery whose root remained inscribed in the book of Tefut.

In the plain, spittle and polluted river water with feces and urine floating across its top, frequently served as replacement for mother's milk. Too malnourished to produce food for her newborn, it was all many a mother had to offer her child. Mothers whose breasts produced milk were given alpha status; babies took turns at their full, sagging breasts that were reminiscent of large coconut being passed around at a noonday meal. Alpha mothers were given first choice to sit beneath the drab shade of the acacia trees. They were first to walk, their feeble knees struggling to carry their scrawny frame, into the muddy river. They were first to drink from and bathe their children in this same polluted water, its flow ebbing toward the Gihon and Southern Nile.

No one knew that mosquito larvae which became the insect that injected them with malaria with a single bite, incubated in the river. Community members stooped in the cool water and hid their shoulders beneath the surface, from the scorching sun, the fiery red star that stood amid more than 100 billion other stars as the largest object in the galaxy, a star that seemed to point its rays directly at Guwati, sending temperatures soaring beyond 120 degrees. Days later malaria swept through the region as if carried on the end of a broom; it took with it mothers, fathers, siblings, friends and ability to see a way out of the death- hole that spanned thirty miles.

Here, in Guwati, no smoke whirled out of roof

tops; strong scent of coffee was absent from doorways. Except for the occasional flames moving away from burning meat, nothing in the sky hinted at life. Five long huts made of bundled grass, sticks and mud sheltered the community from heavy rains. Yet, temperatures soaring and rain forsaking the area, adults and children lived, both day and night, beneath the acacia trees sprawled about the plain. They had lived beneath the shade of the trees for several months, since the rain stopped falling.

Technology had not yet found its way to this plain. Bikila, the community leader, served as compass; tall and stout, Bikila, his skin darker than the cocoa Ethiopia served the international community, told his followers determinedly that what he saw was all there was. He spoke of memories of how life used to be when he was a boy admiring his father's inner focus, decorated spear, quick hands and swift feet, a time when cocoa, sorghum, bananas, maize, wheat, barley,

teff, and millet populated Guwati to overflowing, until

as a boy he thought the produce would go on forever, waiting, tall and healthy like the grass, to be picked. His father's heroism worked a power stronger than blood into Bikila. Faithful to his oft- spoken commands Bikila's followers needed his memories.

At the edge of the plain, toddlers clung to the backs of their parents as if hiding from death. Human skeletons, protruding at the joints the way buoys bob above the surface of ocean water, covered the earth. The souls who once lived in these bones, who once sent bodies dancing, walking, running and soaring with passion long enough to make more babies that would die at the fierce blow of malaria and starvation, made the area heavy. Even without the bodies that once held them, the souls could not get free. They put a weight in the area where the skeletons lay that could be felt, a weight that was thick like plastic sticking against hot skin, a weight that made it hard to breathe. Toddlers walked around the bones. Their collective gaze locked on the fleshless joints.

Farther away from the toddlers and seeking the

lightness of laughter, older children joined hands and sang songs. Their voices rose with mirth high above the trees, and extended far beyond the plain. Mulukan, a short, inquisitive girl with knots on her elbows and knees and a belly as swollen as her mother's had been when she was nine months pregnant with her, sang loudest. When playing games or hunting into the dirt for bugs to eat like candy, Mulukan endured the scorch of the sun longer than any other child. She was one of the children whose parents and siblings, two sisters and three brothers, physical existence died to the bite of hungry male lions, heat or the malaria.

No one took her into their kin-group. She simply mixed in with the other children the way paper blows into trees and grass on a windy day. When her mother's body went to the malaria, Mulukan started sleeping on the ground at the ends of an older girl's feet. When no one kicked or shooed her away; she called that place at the end of the older girl's feet *aqal* or home.

Last night, several hours after Mulukan's

mother died, pygmy kingfishers, small, brightly colored birds Mulukan's mother used to leave insects and crumbs of food for, sang from the top of an acacia tree. Before daybreak threatened to lighten the sky, the pygmy kingfishers flew out of the tree. With each flap of their wings, the birds took higher elevation, until soon they were gone from the plain.

The weather was balmy, the moon white. It was as if the heavens were thanking the community for letting them take Mulukan's mother back, back into the sky, far above the trees, the moon, the stars, everything the community could see. Yards away from the tree the pygmy kingfishers once perched in, mosquitoes circled the mound of dirt where Mulukan's mother's body lay.

A sizable distance away from the dirt mound, Mulukan, her eyes heavy with sleep, her mind burdened with loss, saw an apparition. The vision was so clear and potent it was as if Mulukan's spirit draped her petite body with fatigue, the way a surgeon stilled a patient's body with anesthesia, just so it could operate. Dark went across the sky. Mulukan's limbs were heavier than they had been hours ago. Her chest rose and fell in a slow, methodic rhythm. It was then her spirit showed her what she would never see with the eyes filling her head, the eyes her mother told her were 'sweet brown', the head her siblings laughed about, pointed at and pronounced, "*sana kubwa.*"

Her mother stood at her side. Not a hint of malaria shadowed her; she was strong. She whispered, "Mulukan, you are a triumphant teacher. You will lead a nation." Then like death itself, the bitter fixation that took her mother away from her, the vision was gone.

During the burial earlier in the day, the men in the plain, their painted bodies long and thin like the sticks they carried, moved the dirt over Mulukan's mother's body, filling the hole they'd dug hours before, the hole Mulukan's mother's body now lay at the bottom of, as the fire-hot rays drenched Mulukan's skin from the sun which seemed to be pointed right at her. The dance, sway and singing of the women who stood so close to her she felt their skin pushing into hers while her mother's body was being buried – it all drained Mulukan; she drifted into deeper sleep with ease. The further fatigue carried her into sleep's portal, the tighter disbelief grabbed at the vision. A dream, a dream, Mulukan told herself while she moved away from spirit-talk, the flutter of her eyelids slowing.

When the sun shone in the sky and the vision seemed make-believe, Mulukan shook off sleep and called out, "Mother." Sadness covered her like a heavy blanket."Mother," she called. All that came back to her was the sound of dirt blowing across the earth. She lay in the fetal position. She was six years old. Her life filled with so much pain she forgot how to cry, but that's what she felt like doing.

When Mulukan's people arrived at the plain in Guwati, Ethiopia, Africa's oldest independent country, all of the adults bore a deep tribal marking at the center of their forehead, a marking made with the searing edge of a sharp knife. When they first arrived at the plain, the grass was green and leaves on the trees were full. The land, though flat for miles except for one steep, lone hill, danced with acacia trees, yellow daisies, purple dolichos, and pink orchards. Since the men were herdsmen, cattle, camel and sheep huddled at the edges of the plain. Occasionally a few chickens clucked their way into the area.

Within hours of arriving to the plain the men erected the grass, stick and mud huts which the women filled with hand-carved, cooking utensils and floor mats for sleeping. The river was clean. It gurgled while it moved over the rocks decorating its bed.Wattled Ibis, Abyssinian long-claw, pygmy kingfishers and yellow throated seed-eaters flew across the sky. The sound of their loud, beckoning calls echoed throughout the area. At that time, in the plain, a thing called malaria, a disease that, globally, claims one child every thirty seconds, did not exist. Babies laughed and cooed.

Men came over the hill with deer, hen and a

18

rare buffalo hoisted on their strong shoulders; they carried enough food for the community to feast on for days. All the mothers' breasts gifted their children with milk. Then suddenly the rainfall ceased, temperatures escalated, water muddied and flies and mosquitoes swarmed the river and trees. "Dead ancestors coming back to settle the score," women said, blaming the brutal weather change on angry ancestral spirits called forth by meanness crafted in the hearts of a few unforgiving men in their community, men who struck their wives and children until they bled, men who kept their brows furrowed and tight.

As if spooked by the mosquitoes, the cattle, camel and sheep moved in herds across the plain. The last time Mulukan saw the animals, they were ascending the steep hill that seemed to go on forever. Mulukan stood gape-eyed and watched the animals go over the hill. She wanted to go with them. Even now, away from the people who sat beneath the acacia trees, Mulukan stood at the edge of the plain staring at the hill.

"What are you doing?" Bikila, dreams of his father fading, his brown eyes dreary, his body yelping for food that could not be found, called out to her. Moving beyond his four wives, he leaned forward and examined Mulukan. She upset his peace. Yesterday when her mother died he expected her to fall into another mother's arms and weep. She didn't. He watched her. She didn't cry once. This morning she smiled and played with the other children. It was as if she didn't know her father died nine months earlier, crumpling in a ball after he returned from hunting, his liver and kidneys surrendering to a heatstroke, or that her mother died just the previous afternoon.

Mulukan wasn't like her mother, a woman who had been inconsolable for several days after her husband's death. The day her husband died, Mulukan's mother refused comfort. Three weeks later two of Mulukan's brothers were mauled by hungry male lions. It was then Bikila instructed the people to gather their belongings and prepare to move.

Grass was being eaten up by the sun. It hadn't rained in three weeks. Having seen this cycle of lack, Bikila knew waiting to see what would come of the land would ensure doom. The community covered ten miles before they located an area populated with lush trees. They remained a month, until swarms of mosquitoes chased them out. Before they left, Mulukan's mother, melancholy beginning to attach to her with each departing kin, buried her remaining sons and two eldest daughters after malaria snatched them from her, taking them, one by one, back to the earth.

The women searched for roots in the underbrush, but nothing but death took the fever away from Mulukan's four siblings. Two weeks later, the community settled in the plain where yesterday Mulukan stood next to bare-breasted women, her head brushing their knees, while she watched her mother's body go back to the earth.

Bikila wondered what would come of Mulukan. He regarded her as if she were a book that, if he studied enough, would bring him wisdom. He made note of her conversation, ill- timed laughter and body language. He measured her responses to life events against those of the other children.

The way she dealt with the loss of her family intrigued - frightened him. He began to think there was something sinister about her. It was as if she welcomed suffering, played and laughed with it, made it one of her invisible playmates.

"What are you doing over here by yourself?"

Just as Mulukan went to turn, Bikila was upon her. She felt the heat from his body hovering against her back.

"What are you doing over here?"

Mulukan knew she could be punished, sharp blows coming down upon her shoulders like heavy logs, if she didn't turn and face him. Yet she kept her back to him. "Watching the hill."

He followed her pointing finger then laughed. "Silly girl," he said then he turned and walked away from her.

She didn't move except to lower her arm.

"Come on," he demanded.

She stood with her back to him. He responded by rushing to her side and grabbing her arm. She grimaced while his long, dirty fingernails dug like thick, sharp pins into her skin. She didn't move.

With a hard shove, he freed himself from her and stormed across the plain. As soon as he neared a group of women, he lashed out at them for not watching after Mulukan, for not training her to be a good woman.

Feeling the sting of embarrassment his harsh words brought them, residue of spit that had flown out of his mouth while he shouted at them yet on their faces, two of the women stood and neared Mulukan. Once at

her side, they slapped her face several times – hard

- then grabbing her arms and squeezing them so she could not gain freedom, they dragged her back to the tree where they had previously rested.

The following morning, two days after her mother's body went back to the earth, a strong wind that blew against and tumbled tree leaves brought Mulukan courage. It woke her with its shrill whistling. No one else stirred. Mulukan was light on her feet while she hurried across the plain, her gaze fixed on the hill.

Sound of impending rain covered her footsteps. She knew the community would awaken soon, morning wrestling them away from the serenity of sleep. Cooler temperatures and the hint of rain would decorate their faces with smiles. They might not look for her straightaway. She almost sang while she ran down the hill.

Chapter Two

Desire and intrigue were not the best advisers, Mulukan discovered four days later. She knew the community had searched diligently for her. She imagined the mothers mourning her loss. The children likely told themselves she had gone the way of the earth. Now crumpled on her side against the dry ground, she told herself she had run into the arms of death. In every direction she looked there was nothing but dirt. The sun beat upon her like an angry man hitting her with a hammer just come out of an oven.

Dirt coated her throat and made it hard for her to breathe. The beetles she'd caught with the ends of her fingers yesterday then bit down on, chewing them like they were tiny bits of gum before she swallowed, turned her stomach. She gagged then caught the vomit before it spewed out of her dry, crusty mouth. Vomit again in her stomach, she smiled. The vomit tasted good going down her throat. Swallowing it reminded her of times when her father brought them enough food to eat for days. While she lay against the dirt, red ants and euryopis splendens, small spiders that lived above ground, crawled onto her skin and into her hair.While the insects moved over her, their thin legs beginning to stir with haste, Mulukan recalled how moist the air had been the early morning she ran away from the plain; she knew rain had come. With the rain was green foliage for the ground, berries to the trees, cleaner water and the return of livestock.

Mulukan wrestled beneath the thin layer of sleep. She kicked, slugged death, and gulped air. Her stomach, dirt and ants filling her navel, ceased to ache. She had grown accustomed to starvation's familiar sting. Her young heart, straining under the pressure of her thinning, malnourished blood, had learned to beat with the smallest amounts of oxygen.

Mulukan's eyelids quivered. While she lay on her side with her eyes closed and her conscious mind tucked deep inside a dream, a woman, her body decorated in a long, flowing black and red dress, stood next to her. In her hand was a spear; its top end was sharp. It glistened as if hungry for prey. "Amazon Warrior," Mulukan whispered. Her breath went out with a flutter. She'd heard the stories; her mother told them – stories about African women who could not be defeated.

Her dreaming mind scanned the woman's countenance and the stories her mother told her stretched out like the empty earth. Mulukan leaped off the ground in her dream - and at first she moved back, away from the woman. Then she moved toward the woman as if to embrace her.

The woman pushed Mulukan's hands away and stepped back. Her heels dug into the earth with her biting refusal to be touched. "You are a mighty warrior."

Struck hard by the woman's refusal to embrace her, Mulukan stirred in her sleep. In her dream she lowered her head and stared at the ground. When she looked up, the woman was gone.

Half an hour passed before Mulukan woke.

When she did she squatted and urinated the way she always did when she woke. Her bladder empty and memory of the sleep induced vision of the woman gone into the wind, Mulukan started walking. The spiders and ants shook at the effort of her moving feet; some of the insects dropped off her body to the ground.

Two miles later, Mulukan's knees buckled; she fell into the dirt. Her arms went out, her legs back, the way a bird's legs and wings go in different directions seconds before the bird takes flight. Mulukan's heart spoke to the sky and told it to bring relief; the pain of being a motherless child in a big world made her feel like she was drowning. To six-year old Mulukan, the sky was Yhwh and she could not suffer another step.She lay against the earth for hours, long enough for the sky to turn white with heat.

When she raised her head, a raven, its thick, black beak closed and pointed away from her, stood at her side. Because she too was small, the bird looked huge to Mulukan. She hurried to her feet and ran from

28

the bird, up a hill. Her heart pounded in her chest; it beat so fast Mulukan thought it was trying to beat its way out of her body. The raven crowded her thoughts with fear and dread; she kept looking over her shoulder while she ran. Her eyes had widened with the expanse of fright. Then, and as if the ground had opened beneath her, she lost her footing. Her shoulders ached, her knees felt like they would loosen from their sockets while she rolled to the bottom of the hill. She almost cursed the bird. Moments later, when her body stilled, she stretched out her hands and looked up in surprise when she touched wood.

"Come along, Abayomi. Come along." "But, Father."

"Come along."

"How much for these shoes?"

Voices. Mulukan listened from where she lay behind a tall, wood produce stand, the place where she landed after she rolled to the bottom of the hill. From where she lay behind the stand, she watched feet, some belonging to children, others belonging to adults, move back and forth in front of the small open space at the bottom of the stand. Behind her was only dirt and open sky. She appeared alone except for the hurrying feet and the rainbow voices – so many voices.

"How far along in school is the youngest one? She is growing so fast."

"I know, like a vine. She just keeps going up-up."

"Special! Special! Special! Come and take advantage of these many specials we have on all kinds of fruit and vegetables. You'll be glad you did. Don't go home without some of these delicious foods."

Mulukan peered up. Her thoughts were on the energy in the rainbow voices. Her eyes widened. It was so close, a market. It brimmed with people, some fat, some thin, none starving.

Mulukan crawled to the edge of the stand and peered around the corner. She watched the people and searched for an opening, a time when she could mix in with them undetected. That time did not come until nightfall. Everyone, except for one man, was gone away from the market. The juice of squashed tomatoes, melons, greens and beets sprinkled the earth. The man packed up the last supplies of his fruit and vegetable stand. Mulukan ran up to him like she was his daughter, like he'd been looking for her.

Dirt filled her matted hair and covered her limbs. Dried snot clung to her lip. Flies circled her groin. Her knees and eyes were swollen. Her stomach, protruding like an empty bowl, went out to the man and asked for food. Mulukan – as if she'd always been happy, gave him her best smile. When he smiled back at her, her jaws fattened with mirth.

"Lost from your parents?" the man asked while he searched her face for answers, for clues that revealed the reason she was at the market at this late hour alone. Despite the clues, not once did he allow himself to believe she could be one of the millions of children death had pushed out into the street absent their parents. AIDS had been the dominant disease

31

ripping parents from their children this time. But there had always been a vicious disease ravaging parts of Africa for as long as the man could recall. Once, to distance himself from the hurt, the insanity of tragedy, he ceased reading stories about countless children roaming Africa alone, unsure of which direction to move in, roaming through life as if just by walking, they would find safety, a place to lay their heads, a place devoid of heartache. For so long, he wouldn't look at the children. He refused their large, brown eyes.

Two years ago he and his wife of thirty-eight years lived on a large farm. The earth always pushed up produce like goodness coming straight from Yhwh, the only source in the universe that flows, the source many call love. Abandoned children showed up at their front gate each morning. A year later, the circle of starvation and desperation still revealing itself on the children's dirty, worn, tired faces, and his wife went insane. The desperation the children brought to the gate each morning cursed her with melancholy.

It happened slowly, very slowly, as if it weren't happening at all. At first his wife, her eyes having become sullen like the children's, begged him with, "We have to do more for them." Weeks later she fed the children from the harvest they had planned to sell at the market, currency with which they would pay their household expenses.

"We cannot do this," the man would tell her while light from their bedroom lamp flickered across the room. But her guilt that they lived inside the comforts of a large farm, her guilt that they had plenty to eat and wear while hundreds of children outside their home had only what she handed them through the open space in the front gate - that guilt drove her insane.

Months after the children showed up, she took to staring into space, her gaze landing on nothing in particular. She mumbled to herself; the man saw her lips moving as if she were talking to someone, but when he looked about, there was no one else. As if it would halt the onslaught of insanity that was

33

beginning to overtake his wife, that was beginning to drown her, he went into town and bought five acres of land.

Deed in hand, he opened the gate and standing amid the children like a sergeant, asked, "Who knows how to farm?" Three hands, their ends badly chewed, their palms as brown as their backs, went up. "Who would like to learn how to farm?" his voice boomed. His gazed darted and searched their faces. Every hand sprang into the air. With a jerk of his head and a swing of his arm he called out, "Follow me." At the edge of the five acres of land, he stopped. "This land is more than enough to feed all of you."

His wife wasn't alive to witness the first full harvest come in. By that time she had locked herself in their barn and slit her wrists. When he found her that evening she was already dead. While family and friends and the children, some of them fat, surrounded the large hole he was soon to place her body inside and cover with dirt, the bed of the earth, the substance that helped feed the children, he talked to his wife.

"See what your desperation has done for the children?"

"And where are you from?" the man asked Mulukan.

With a twist of her ankle, she pulled her hands behind her back and looked up at him. There was enough dirt on her face and body to clog a narrow drainage pipe. While he looked at her he wondered if she was ill. Her hair though dry and brittle, was dark and healthy. Her eyes were clear.

"Mother," he tried, Mulukan yet silent. He turned and grabbed a peach. "Here," he told her with a smile on his face and his arm extended toward her.

She took the strange fruit inside her hand.

He watched her bite into the fruit then consume it recklessly. Finished eating the fruit's flesh she bit at the seed. When the seed didn't crack, she stuck it in her jaw and sucked it. She stared longingly at the row of peaches behind the man.

"Do you understand what I'm saying?" he

35

asked Mulukan while he turned and started placing the last remaining pieces of fruit onto a wheeled cart. When his stand was empty and clean, he pushed the cart close to a blue and yellow truck.

When he turned, Mulukan was gone. He'd given her a bag of peaches, a bag of green beans, corn and a jug of water. He told her to put the vegetables over fire, but because he doubted she spoke the same tongue he did, he imagined she would eat the corn and green beans straight out of the bag. After he looked over the market to ensure Mulukan wasn't hiding, he climbed inside his truck and drove to the end of the road. At the end of the road, he turned left and drove around the corner.

Chapter Three

Two weeks later and a town over from where she met the man at the market, Mulukan stayed close to people's voices, as though following a compass. Wayward men grabbed her arm and tried to force her into dark, narrow passageways, but she kicked, bit them and freed herself from their grasp. The memory of the man from the market two weeks gone, the thought to return to the fruit and vegetable stand nipped at her, but she swatted at the thought until it left her.

Where the thought went she did not know; she only knew she no longer wrestled with it. She was alone, yet she kept moving. Her feet headed in the direction she set out for early that dawn three weeks ago when she walked away from the only people she'd ever known – the community she'd been born into. She refused to venture away from the path the hill had set her upon.

"Little girl."

Mulukan looked the man in the face. Then she lowered her gaze. The man's eyes bred trouble. When she looked at him her soul hurt. She moved away from him in slow backward steps. His gaze remained upon her. Across from where they stood, drivers in small cars with the windows rolled down, and drivers in trucks with wobbly wheels and beds filled with boxes of produce or old furniture, puttered down an unpaved street. On both sides of the street were rows of small wood houses.

Amid the traffic and houses, Mulukan searched for adults she could scream to for help. She also hunted for large objects she could grab and throw at the man. When she felt the man closing the distance that separated them, she started running. She ran until her breath thickened and her heart raced. She didn't stop running until she looked up and saw a woman sitting at the edge of a blue wood house. Children danced and played near the woman's feet.

The man, his head bowed more with regret than shame, turned and walked toward the other end of the street.

"Hey," the woman called out, her fingers working at the straw of a new basket, when Mulukan moved away from her.

Mulukan met the woman's glance.

"You're not from around here, are you?" Before Mulukan answered, the woman looked toward the other end of the street where the strange man had once stood. Seeing him no more, she called Mulukan over to her with a swing of her arm. "Stay away from him. He chooses not to do good. I don't care what he offers you, stay away from him." She shook her head and fixed a hard look on her face. "No good. He doesn't do good." She shook her head again. "He doesn't do good."

Even though the woman had not asked her if she'd like to mix in with the other children and become a part of the fabric of her life, Mulukan asked, "Can I stay with you tonight? I'll be gone before the sun shows in the sky." She peered down the street, in the direction where the man had once stood. "Is he out early?"

A chuckle brightened the woman's plump face. "No. He drinks heavy. He doesn't come out until about this time every day. You'll be good leaving early in the morning. And," she added while she extended her hand toward Mulukan, "My name is Desta." She looked at Mulukan's sad eyes and knew the child standing before her was one of Africa's many orphans, another child death had pushed into the street alone.

Without another word spoken between them they sealed the agreement, and Mulukan stayed the night. She washed her hair twice, scrubbed beneath her fingernails, took her fingers and scraped and scrubbed her teeth. That night for the first time in her life she was given a mattress to sleep on and a bedroom to sleep in.

As soon as she sat on the mattress of the bed next to the window, she sprang to her feet. The tiny braids in her hair, worked there with her own narrow fingers the day before her mother's body returned to the earth, flew into the air then came down about her head like a bundle of black shoe strings.

The other six children who sat on the bed with Mulukan laughed. A tall, wiry girl with thick braids and a broad smile, oldest of the children, asked Mulukan why she leaped from the bed. "I've never slept on the soft thing before," Mulukan told her. "I thought I was going to fall through the floor."

The children fastened their attention upon Mulukan and, their eyes ballooning, they stared at her. They wondered what it was about the strange girl sitting on the edge of the bed that kept her from sleeping the way they always had. Before they could press Mulukan with questions, their mother opened the bedroom door. Peering inside, she smiled and asked, "Everyone all right?"

Mulukan scarcely heard her, but her smile – that Mulukan took in fully, completely. Desta's smile pulled Mulukan toward its warmth and made her want to run across the room and hug Desta, but something kept Mulukan pinned to the bed. Mulukan wanted to wrestle free because she wanted to embrace Desta's warm smile, an act that would find her wrapped inside a mother's arms.

The children looked at their mother and grinned. They told her they were fine. Their faces gave her a comforting assurance, although she hadn't poked her head inside the room because she feared something was amiss with them. She stuck her head inside the room because she wanted to check on the little girl whose path crossed hers less than four hours ago. She recalled when she was a child herself and had been placed into a classroom of children who knew each other, had played and laughed together for months, while she was the only child no one knew.

The other children in the classroom stared at her, looked at her as if they could measure her thoughts and the breadth and depth of her heart with their eyes. They looked hard at her. Discomfort came around her like a cloak; she wanted to run. She looked back at the school door, but her feet remained planted. It wasn't until one of the two teachers entered the room, and introducing her, encouraged the children to greet her with a word of hello, a friendly smile and a hug that the ice broke, and she started to feel loved again.

Desta's smile widened when her gaze fell across Mulukan's face. "Have the children told you their names?"

The children looked at each other then, with sheepish grins on their faces, they turned and revealed their names, one by one, to Mulukan.

"My name is Mulukan," she shared in return.

"Would anyone like anything before I turn out the light? I want you all to lie down and get plenty of good rest. Your minds and bodies will thank you all night long, early in the morning and all of tomorrow for having done so."

The way the children smiled up at their mother let Mulukan know she was oftentimes gentle, kind and flexible the way a river doesn't fight rocks it moves over. She wasn't being kind for her sake; this was who she was. Briefly Mulukan remembered her own mother and felt a tinge of envy stab her thoughts. She almost looked at the floor, but her father had taught her to hold her head high so many times, she was unable to. She looked from Desta to Desta's six children. "I'm fine," she finally said.

Desta stuck her head further inside the room. One of the children, a small boy named Berta, was crouched on the floor behind the door. He played with a beetle. "And the rest of you?" she asked for confirmation that the children were fully prepared to climb into bed and fall fast asleep.

Berta reluctantly moved his attention from the reddish orange beetle to his mother. He presented her a snaggle-toothed grin.

His grin said it all, and before Desta pulled the door closed, she gently told the children, "Good night. Talk and listen to Yhwh before you fall asleep and have a wonderful night of rest."

Mulukan listened while Desta's feet moved

away from the door. The light out, the children hurried to recline on the two beds in the room. The four boys remained in the bed next to the window while the two girls crossed the floor and slept in the bed closest to the door.

But Mulukan stood next to the door with her hands behind her back. After the children were in their beds for several seconds, she started swaying from side to side. She had never slept standing up before, but she was willing to try. Desta having served her and each of the children a hot plate of hen smothered in gravy, garlic mashed potatoes and asparagus, Mulukan's body was regaining strength. The only thing she thought would get in the way of her standing all night were her legs; she imagined that, in time, they would tire, then start to ache. Beyond that, she figured she could lean against a wall and sleep until the sun yawned in the sky.

Abeba, a girl nearly a foot shorter than Mulukan propped herself up on an elbow, scooted over and patted the newly created empty space on the side of the bed she slept in with her older sister who had already begun to drift into a restful sleep. "Come on," Abeba said, her voice rising and sounding like a small bird or a squeaking mouse. "Come sleep with us. Just come on," she said again, pulling Mulukan toward her with the sound of her voice and the curl of her small hand. "We want you to sleep with us. You help us catch up to the boys. Because of you, now there are three of us."

Mulukan went slowly across the floor and climbed into bed with the two sisters. She lay down on the edge of the bed next to Abeba who talked to her until she drifted off to sleep.

"Where are you from?" Abeba whispered.

Although happy with Abeba's acceptance of her, Mulukan wanted to embrace silence. She wanted to lie on her back and enjoy the comforts of sleeping on a mattress for the first time in her life. She wanted to stare up at the ceiling and watch passing light, coming away from cars and trucks driving on the street, flicker, dance and move across the ceiling.

"The plain."

"Where is that?"

"Over the hill."

"The hill outside?"

"No. It's a hill far from here."

"What's in the plain?"

"People." Mulukan paused. "A tribe. The tribe that I am from is in the plain. They were there when I left, and," she smiled. "It rained the day I left. I felt the rain in the air. Rain brings food. Rain makes crops grow. It also brings the animals back."

"I like to climb trees," Abeba said. "I climb them and I look down on my mother and father and brothers and sister and friends. Sometimes I climb--"

"Where is your father?" Mulukan asked. She had never seen a healthy family absent either a woman or a man.

Abeba giggled. "He works in the country. He comes home on weekends. He keeps us fed. He cares for us." After she took in a breath, Abeba continued her discussion of trees. "Sometimes I climb the tree at the edge of the school and watch teachers inside their classrooms. It's fun. I can see a lot when I'm up in a tree."

"Can you hear them when they talk?" Mulukan asked.

Abeba propped herself on an elbow and looked at Mulukan. When she returned to her back she laughed innocently. "Trees don't talk."

"Why do you climb them then?"

The question caught Abeba by surprise. "That's what I mean," Mulukan said. She folded her arms and fastened them behind her neck. Her smile widened. "They talk to you." She gazed up at the ceiling. "My father and mother told me." After a brief pause, she added, "The trees don't actually talk. Yhwh talks to you through the trees. Anything that has life in it, Yhwh moves through, because Yhwh is life. My father and mother told me." She clasped her hands together and gave a sure smile. The room was silent then Mulukan turned and smiled right at Abeba. "Like when you were nice to me."

The two girls smiled at each other until warmth covered their bodies like extra skin. "Anything with life in it shares life with you. Yhwh is always sharing." Mulukan's smile broadened. "That's why you like to climb into trees. Trees live long. They know a lot." Looking at Abeba, she asked, "Do you ask them questions?"

"If I don't think they talk, why would I ask them a question?"

Mulukan laughed.

Abeba and Mulukan continued to lay side by side looking into each other's faces. "Do you ask the trees questions, Mulukan?"

"I ask Yhwh the questions. My father and mother told me that life only comes from Yhwh, and nothing else. But, for me, a lot of times the answer comes while I'm near a tree."

"What do you ask?"

"Which way to go next."

"How would trees know that?"

Mulukan raised then lowered her shoulders. "They don't. Yhwh does. I don't know how it happens. It just does. Yhwh moves through the tree, like Yhwh moves through people and anything else that's alive. I ask people which way to go next too, and," she added, "I knew that hill back in the plain was telling me something and all those animals going over that hill." She paused. "I knew. I could feel it." She raised then lowered her shoulders again. "Trees, like people, have life in them. Life has the answer. Yhwh is life."

"You're alive."

Mulukan was silent. The words went into her like more pigment going into her skin.

"You can't stay a little girl. We're going to become a woman."

"Then we're going to become old women."

"Mothers maybe."

"And aunts."

"Grandmothers."

"Wow."

"Then old like you said, really old, not old like my mother is now."

"How old is your mother?"

"I don't know."

"Is she as old as that tree by your house?"

"I don't know." Abeba laughed. "I wasn't here when my mother was born."

"You're right," Mulukan conceded.

"Did mothers used to be little girls?"

It was Mulukan's turn to laugh. "Yes."

Chapter Four

Dew clung to the warm earth the way frost stuck to the ground in winter, but night had removed itself from the village. Birds chirping in the tree near the house Mulukan slept in awakened neighboring residents to what they considered to be the start of the day. Some of the houses, with huge chimneys crowning their tops, whisked the strong scent of coffee, morning's liquid gold, beneath the noses of more than half the people who lived on the street.

Children slept through the scent as if nestled inside the arms of an angel. Adults who drank coffee but who hadn't yet risen from bed, stirred almost at once. Dogs ambled away from slumber with a shake of their tails and a yelp, a request for food and the freedom to come indoors to the shelter of their keepers' home.

In the house Mulukan slept in, silence webbed its way through every room. Licking her dry lips and blinking crust off her lashes, Mulukan stared across the room. Like a drunken woman, she struggled to focus. Her vision blurred; everything in the room seemed to be moving. She did manage to see the woman standing in front of her. She had her mother's face. Like the dew on the earth, a cloud of mist surrounded the woman. Mulukan rubbed her eyes. She told herself the woman was a 'talking cloud'.

Placing a finger against her mouth, the woman encouraged Mulukan to keep silent. "You were right about the things you told the girl." Seeing questions hovering in Mulukan's face, she added, "You are my daughter and I am your mother."

Mulukan reached out to touch the spirit bearing her mother's face. Her hand went straight through the woman. Yet she knew her mother was there, standing in front of her. No body trapped her or held her hostage to repetitive thoughts and emotions. Her mother was free, more alive than she had been back in the plain.

"Others are awakening." The spirit bearing Mulukan's mother's face smiled. "Some of them want to bless the way you do. Some want to curse; they think it will rid them of pain. They are wrong. Each breath is love; each step is peace. You are being prepared to deal with the hardness of what you have to do." She stood back and smiled over her daughter. "You are ready. Mulukan, you will be a woman soon. You must remember that you are a queen, a leader of nations. You will help people heal. Yhwh is always with you." She paused. "I am always with you." She kissed her daughter. When she did Mulukan closed her eyes; the kiss felt like a butterfly had gently brushed her face. "I know you enjoy the comforts here, Mulukan, but you cannot stay here. You must keep moving." Just as Mulukan opened her eyes, her mother blended in with the yellow paint decorating the room, the air Mulukan and the other children breathed, the tree at the edge of the house.

Section II

To evolve we must experience change.

Chapter Five

Time changed Mulukan. Her once flat chest expanded into a mound of malleable flesh, a thing that caused men to gape at her. Her hips widened; her thighs were taut and full. Her spine and limbs lengthened making her six feet tall. Her lips, ripe like summer melons, were supple and full. Her wide, curious eyes looked like they were in bloom. Her laugh was deeper . . . richer. Her voice, deferring to circumstance, changed like a wind instrument; oft times it was strong and deep. Over the years, her voice, her firm, gentle handshake and unmovable belief that Yhwh loved her gained her a trio of jobs: cook at a restaurant in Addis Ababa; accountant with the Parliament of Ethiopia; and communications writer at the Office of Government Spokesperson.

Away from work, Mulukan gave herself to research. Restoring Africa was a hunger grafted to her heart.

The hunger, filling her, pinning her with ache at the plight of Africa's citizens, came at her the way the mosquitoes bearing malaria had years ago when she lived amongst the community in the plain. She didn't realize it until now, but each step she took in effort to walk up, walk away from hunger, pain, ache and death led her here. It was not enough that she had again crossed paths with the farmer she met at the market, the man with the blue and yellow truck, less than a week after she left Desta's home in the village, the small tree keeping sentry over Desta's house, watching out for her and her four sons and two daughters.

It was not enough that she had lived on the five acre farm the man from the market owned, pieces of her life becoming a thread of the farmer's personal history, blending with the other children who had come to the farm hungry, at the edge of death due to starvation. It was not enough that she had attended to academic study diligently while she lived on the farm for ten years until she enrolled at university.

It was not enough. Mulukan was the little girl from the plain, the child Bikila thought would never fit in, her heart staying open like a bowl always turned up. Mulukan was the little girl from the plain; ghosts from the skeletons she once stared at on the hot earth, malaria and hot-heat soaking their dry bones, moved like shadows across her grown woman face. They whispered to her things about her mother, things she had forgotten, like the sound of her mother's laughter, its volume pitching and falling like the river water that ebbed toward the Great Nile. They flashed images of her father's face, his brow tight from hours of toiling for food, hunting big game with other men in the community. Her ancestors, their skeletons buried deep beneath the earth back in the plain would not let her forget, that she was Mulukan, the little girl from the plain, the child who had once been so hungry she lost the strength to continue the long walk up.

Mulukan's hunger for food had gone deeper

than her bone, far into her spirit, beyond the reach of genocide, fear and tribal wars. Mulukan's hunger had grown up with her, expanding as each new inch widened her thighs, filled her buttocks, made her chest go out, as if seeking friends, as if calling natives to her, closer to her chest, to the hunger in her heart. Mulukan's hunger for restoring Africa worked like a magnet and pulled people like Kokumuo Kenyatta into her days.

The way a baby doesn't know it's aging even while it evolves from laying against its mother's soft breasts to crawling to walking to making early attempts at running, Mulukan didn't know Kokumuo would lead her to the man who would give her the great lessons on Africa, lessons that dug to the heart of the continent, unearthing truths previously buried beneath generations of colonialism, fear and abuse. The lessons at times would come from books but most often they came from the teacher's mouth. The lessons poured gratitude and joy over Mulukan like a warm shawl covering her skin.

During her first accidental meeting with Kokumuo, Mulukan was mesmerized. Initially scheduled to meet with an older statesman regarding an opening in the Marketing Department, she never meant to interview for the communications writer position at the Office of Government, but when she landed in the interview room Kokumuo, not the elder statesman, showed up. Kokumuo's large brown eyes, his long, lean frame made strong via tri-weekly visits to the gym, and his full smooth mouth arrested Mulukan's attention during their first meeting.

The way Kokumuo carried his body, the fluid motions in his limbs when he crossed the floor and neared her side, gave out an air of confidence that reminded Mulukan of the sure way the Nile, earth's longest river, went over a bed of earth. The tenderness in Kokumuo's smile cut away at the callous that had grown through the teen years on Mulukan's heart. Kokumuo's smile made Mulukan long to trust again the way she had trusted her father, her mother, her siblings and those back in the plain who transmitted enough courage to always be gentle. Kokumuo's smile pushed desire into Mulukan; his smile made Mulukan seek to trust when there was no work to do, trust when there was no one for her to save or carry to fresh water.

When Kokumuo neared her side, Mulukan saw her hands shake. She felt emotion go like a ball into her throat. It was all Mulukan could do to stop staring at Kokumuo's well manicured hands, his broad shoulders and chiseled chin. And when he started talking, his milky voice almost coaxed her to sleep until he spoke about the man she would write press releases, speeches, lengthy reports and statistical data for.

That man was Abasi Nyathi, the President of Mariami. He was a giant of a man in stature and in spirit. His frame stretched six feet, nine inches long. His girth, though wide, was muscular. He too frequented the gym, often going to the private health club on the third floor of the main complex where his office was located. More frequently than not, Kokumuo accompanied him on those visits to the gym. The two men strained, grunted and pushed up weights on a myriad of nautilus machines, ran several laps around the indoor track and sat for half an hour in the sauna, the heat cleansing their pores and softening their skin.

At first Mulukan feared she'd never fit into Kokumuo and President Nyathi's schedules, the two men having obviously bonded well over the previous five years they'd worked together, but they took to her the way her brothers had when she was a small girl playing within the reach of her father's and mother's watchful eyes. It was Kokumuo who taught Mulukan the art of speech and press release writing, a skill she discovered required near as much imagination as fact finding. He stayed close to her, making sure she knew how to reach him should she need assistance with a project that was turning out to be more challenging than fulfilling.

The first two months she worked at the Office

of Government, he accompanied her to lunch each day and occasionally escorted her to weekend Arts events. While they rounded corners and moved slowly behind the other art gazers led through the gallery by an expert tour guide, Kokumuo, whispering close to Mulukan's ear, pointed at pieces of art then went on to share deeper history, facts the guide hadn't given them, behind the work with her. He knew so much sometimes just being with him made Mulukan feel small. Yet, he wasn't condescending; his conversations were replete with energy, vigor, humility and honesty. He was grateful for Mulukan's company. As he told her countless times the first week she worked at the office, she rescued him from sixteen-hour workdays and six- day workweeks.

On a suffocating hot day in June, more than a year after Mulukan started working at the Office of Government, as it had at least once a day, Monday through Friday, for more than a year, Kokumuo's long shadow appeared in Mulukan's office doorway. The urgency he felt didn't reveal itself on his countenance, but his heart beat wildly in his chest. Having spoken with her earlier about a report she was compiling data for, he gave no introduction to his announcement, words he was certain would send Mulukan reeling. "President Nyathi has taken ill."

The pen Mulukan held as she edited the final draft of President Abasi Nyathi's speech landed against the ruled pad and rolled to the edge of her mahogany desk. It was hard to move; the enemy she feared most, death, was yet again upon the door, threatening to snatch away another chunk of her heart.

Kokumuo stepped beneath the door archway and rounded the corner. The office was so large he didn't see Mulukan until he was halfway inside the office. Scent of new polish pricked his nose. Weeks ago he had a long discussion with Mulukan about purchasing more office furniture; she disregarded his hidden plea for comfort. Except for the mahogany desk, its matching chair, one lamp, a tall wastebasket, and an unframed photo of a hill, blades of burnt grass placed sparsely amid rows of dirt, cattle bordering the steepest parts of the hill and a lone raven perched atop one of the highest limbs of a small acacia tree, there was nothing else in the office. Mulukan asked that the floor remain bare; she liked to listen to the log- drum sound people's feet made when they neared her side.

Walking to the edge of Mulukan's desk, Kokumuo looked her squarely in the eyes. "You're going to deliver tonight's address." He patted her back before he stepped away from her.

Mulukan sprung from the chair.

"The president said so himself." Silence separated those and Kokumuo's next words. "He was rushed to the hospital."

"From whe—"

"He was playing tennis."

"Wha—"

"You have to do it." A second later, seeing the concern etched across her face, Kokumuo lowered his voice and said, "You can do it, Mulukan." He gave her a sure nod. "You know what to say and you're strong."

He paused and informed her, "You're due center stage in two hours."

Mulukan sat at her desk staring at the final draft of the speech she thought she had been writing for the president of Mariami. More than one hundred thousand people would attend the speech in person, coming in on trucks, over loaded cars and on foot from villages miles away from the capital; millions more would tune in by television and radio. She had carefully written the speech, laboring over each word, to ensure President Nyathi made clear the work he had put in to unite, strengthen and advance Mariami, each of its citizens, all its villages and communities – everyone. Although she had also contributed to a sizable portion of the president's success, thoughts of reading the speech herself caused Mulukan to shudder. She spent the next twenty minutes gazing out the window and asking Yhwh why someone else couldn't address the people of Mariami.

An hour later, Kokumuo neared Mulukan's office door again. He leaned his head against the door before he knocked. He recalled how she nearly froze when he told her the President had taken ill. He was aware of her fear, but he knew coddling her would only heighten her doubt. He told himself to be firm with her, force her to see how prepared she was to deliver tonight's address. After he took in then released a deep breath, he balled his hands and rattled the wood then turned the knob. Seconds later his voice echoed across the office. "We're leaving in twenty minutes. You're on stage in an hour." A moment later she listened to the sound of his feet drum the floor while he exited her office and went shoulders back and head high down the corridor. He had not the slightest doubt that by day's end Mulukan, words riding on the strength in her voice, would send all of Mariami rising to its feet.

Kokumuo gone, Mulukan stood and locked her office door. Then she walked to the center of the office and lowered her body to the floor and extended her legs and arms. Stress from the recently received news made her tired; she drifted to sleep absent struggle. Moments later, when she woke to the sound of Kokumuo drumming the door, she brushed her teeth in the bathroom at the back of the office, splashed water across her face and plaited her hair into a long braid that reached to the middle of her back. Half an hour later, she stood on stage in the direct path of a hot sun.

Before her was an ocean of people, their faces searching her eyes for answers, hope that at this same time next year there would be fewer starving people in the villages at the edges of small towns, that the numbers of schools available for their children to attend and learn at would have increased, that their lives, although not drenched with pain, would be better.

On this day there were four speakers, Mulukan being the main one and the one to speak last. Each speaker's introduction was long. Mulukan cringed while she listened to Kokumuo introduce her. He told the crowd about her parents, people he'd scarcely heard her speak about, people he pieced together while observing Mulukan over the last year. At the end of his introduction Kokumuo gave the crowd an assuring smile and said, "Mulukan's parents knew she was special."

Kokumuo's introduction over, Mulukan stood from the high-back chair. En-route to his seat, Kokumuo bumped her shoulder and grinned, alerting her to the fact that he supported her. Mulukan received his shoulder bump with a slow nod and a series of steps that led her to within inches of the microphones bunched at the center of the podium. The next words she spoke were heard around the world. Tomorrow they would be posted on more than half a million web sites, going out as sound bytes, as bits of verbiage posted on blogs and international news pages. Some of the listeners would take Mulukan's words home, pen them on pages of their journals, tucking them safely inside their memories forever.

Mulukan inhaled and her chest expanded. Scanning the crowd and releasing the breath she began, "Mothers and fathers. Brothers and sisters.

Friends. Four years ago we re-elected our leader, President Abasi Nyathi into office. Today as I stand before you, colleague to each person who spoke before you here today and servant to each of you and the president, I am honored to share with you that together," she waved her hands over the crowd, "we have worked diligently at balancing our budget, and our efforts have paid off. We have eaten away at Mariami's international and domestic debt the way those we were indebted to once tried to eat away at us." She stared into the ebony faces, some of them young and moist, others aged and chafed. In their faces she saw the hope and resiliency that showed on Bikila's hardened face when he was met with a challenge, when his thoughts went fishing for memories of his father's strength, a resource that always seemed to hold up. Although she held distaste for the stern way Bikila had led the community and the way he had dug his fingernails into her arm when she was a child, she now saw Bikila's courage, a resource once hidden from her view beneath Bikila's sharp voice. The sea of people standing before her reminded her of home; though not of her blood, she loved these

people.

Her voice rose. "Each member of President Abasi Nyathi's staff has worked long and tirelessly. We focused daily on eradicating the debt. However," she added, pointing to the crowd. "You drove this financial independence." She pounded her hand on the podium. "You demanded this freedom of us. Because this office serves you, this office heard you. No, no," she said with a shake of her head. "We didn't hear you with fancy words, long, flowery speeches or visits to your villages just so we could shake your hands. No, no," she said, her head shaking again. "We heard you with action."

Applause erupted and thundered across the ground.

"Four years ago, the international bank told us we owed them three hundred million. Although we all know the colonies have yet to pay us for the debt of servitude and ill-gotten gain they heaped upon us, today Mariami owes no international organization a cent." She talked through the rising applause and cheers. "Each burden upon this office is a burden upon you, and you have demanded freedom. Four years ago, our domestic debt reached two hundred million. Today that debt has been completely erased."

Another round of applause went across the ground.

"Mariami is finished paying debts. Mariami is finished making debts. The only debt this nation will owe from this day forward, while this office leads you is the debt to love and the debt to keep you free. And now," she added with a shout, "Let us look to the future."

"Last month we built one hundred clean wells in the country's most remote villages. We repaired thirty roadways and began building fifteen dams that will allow electricity into more homes. We raised our clean air and water guidelines, and I am happy to tell you that all of the government and privately owned businesses have complied. Six months ago we opened more than twenty new schools. This time next year we will have opened another twenty schools. All of our children will be educated. A parent's income will not determine which child learns to read and write."

"Throughout the remainder of this year and next we will begin a program that will allow adults who do not know how to read and write to gain a minimal education free of charge. I encourage you to support our universities and enroll to take a course on farming, business operation, or an enterprise your heart calls you toward. As you create financial strength in your own individual families, Mariami becomes stronger. Don't allow anything to detain you from building a stronger you, a stronger family, a stronger tribe, a stronger village, a stronger us, a stronger Mariami." She opened her hands to the crowd as if biding them to come closer, circle her with their united strength. "We are Mariami."

This time when applause erupted, it didn't cease. "This is your Mariami. This is you. Mariami is you. Mariami is me. Mariami is your mother. Mariami is your father. Mariami is your son. Mariami is your daughter." Raising her hands into the air, she shouted, "We are Mariami, and filled with the power of Yhwh we rise. We rise. We rise. We rise."

Chapter Six

Seven years later, Mulukan sat across from President Nyathi in his large plush office. His heart was strong again after seven years of watchful dieting, prayer and meditation. Outside his office window, Abyssinian catbirds chirped and filled the air with music while they flew across the clear, light blue sky.

President Nyathi leaned back in his black leather chair and pressed the tips of his fingers together. He looked squarely at Mulukan. "You were born to lead."

Mulukan ran her tongue across her top lip. "I'm a writer."

He met her tentative glance and smiled warmly.

She studied his smile, his inherent kindness, with approval. He'd accepted her from the start. She was a young twenty-three years old when she showed up at his office, suit jacket draping her shoulders, a mauve sweater and black skirt covering her frame.

Not even a hint of ridicule at her tattered clothing showed on his face. Even then he saw greatness in her. That evening, after their first meeting eight years ago, when she walked home and retired to her one room flat, she knew their paths were meant to cross. Yet, she could hardly believe it. Here she was working for the president of Mariami. She – a child without

parents or siblings in a country where a large family was viewed with awe. Mulukan – the lone child, the woman on her own.

"Onbil is a beautiful island on Africa's eastern shore. It covers more than 675 square miles and boasts a population of twelve million. You are fluent in all five languages spoken on the island. In fact, one of the languages is your native tongue." His smile expanded; his eyes softened. He looked at her as if he was sharing truths with his own daughter, born of his body, alive with his blood. "Kiswahili, Hausa, Dahalo, Mande, and Somali, your native tongue."

"I know about Onbil," Mulukan offered. Those words spoken, she turned away from him. His trust in her made her feel foreign, unsure of herself. Naked. She turned away in embarrassment. Her gaze was down when she said, "I have worked for you for eight years. I know about every square inch of Africa."

He looked at her back. The blouse she wore was silk, off-white in color. Not a wrinkle showed on it. He almost chuckled. She'd learned how to dress up in the eight years they'd known one another. Her clothes showed none of the spots, wrinkles or holes they had the first day she stood at the edge of his office, her hand extended as if to request his acceptance of her more than to say 'hello'.

She laughed then she turned and faced him again. "Because of you, I know Africa. You love Africa. You love her, don't you?"

A sure nod preceded the declaration. "I do. Africa is different and varied because of its fifty- three nations." His gaze lowered, then went up across the room. He glanced out the window and looked at the sun. "They all blend into one powerful, limitless continent." His focus no longer on the window, he faced her and looked her directly in the eyes.

"More of our leaders must govern better, must serve rather than demand service of others."

"Absolutely," he said with a fervent nod. Family is the root of the tree. All nations sprang from family." He shook his head. "A nation cannot be strong when even one village, tribe or family, just one, is weak. It's why the wise teach love. And you, Mulukan," he paused, "can do that. You, Mulukan."

Section III

"Do not vacillate or you will be left in between doing something, having something and being nothing."

African Proverb (Ethiopia)

Chapter Seven

In Onbil, gated irrigation pipes snaked through the ground like aluminum reptiles and watered farm areas. Clean water wells were built in densely populated communities and villages. Fifty acres of new forest pushed above earth, the trees yet trunks but certain to send their tops toward the heavens. For this, lemur, periwinkle, mongoose and gecko gladly climbed and swung through baobab and octopus trees, their bodies light, heads pushed toward the sky. Two hospitals, their corridors beckoning the ill to heal, and schools, their hallways rich with education, went up, making medical assistance available to all Onbil

78

citizens. Education was a requirement for Onbil residents ages six to fourteen. At the edge of the island off the coast of Mariami were two newly created major landfills. Offsetting the waste collected at the landfills was a national recycling program each of Onbil's villages participated in. These were the first steps Mulukan took to restore Onbil after she, in the nation's first democratic election, unanimously won the office of President.

President Nyathi's public support significantly increased the people of Onbil's trust in Mulukan. His efforts allowed Mulukan to focus on strengthening Onbil, a nation consisting of twelve million men, women and children, a nation rich in orchids, baobab and palm trees, marshland, minerals and wildlife, its animals varied and ancient, some of their fossils as old as the 125 million years the island has existed.

Mulukan and members of the Executive Cabinet raised the lowest economic rung in Onbil, an effort that skyrocketed as the numbers of children and adults who could read and write a minimum of two languages at the ninth grade secondary education levels increased. Government sponsored print and voice ads to teach culture celebration were strategically placed throughout the island. Because the National Assembly diligently investigated interior corruption, fraudulent leaders no longer injected Onbil's business owners with the narcotic of fear.

Determined to fully restore Onbil, Mulukan watched for tides of resistance to this freedom. Despite current local leaders' voiced threats of violence if government handouts and under-the- table deals ceased, Mulukan knew as she and other members of the Executive Cabinet and National Assembly continued to improve the standard of living in Onbil, corruption would cease. Onbil's citizens would come to expect the better way of life and would, in time, refuse to tolerate any level of government corruption.

The road was arduous and, at times, pushed Mulukan to extreme inner fatigue. Her life having been threatened a dozen times, when she ventured into public a convoy of security guards accompanied her. She missed opportunities for solitude, the chance to feel like Onbil's other citizens. Resistance to change was formidable.

More than once Mulukan stood alone while she faced an adversary. Those desperate to overthrow her leadership argued, through media outlets and death threats sent directly to Mulukan's office, that the past was safe. When Mulukan didn't give in to their early threats, they hired rebel fighters, men who swung their fists through the air, raised their voices and demanded Mulukan either leave office or take Onbil back to the way it was before she arrived, a time when corruption was rampant.

Mulukan bore up under their hard faces and their brows tight with rage. The rebels knew with certainty what the past held they screamed amid the spit that flew hot and gritty out of their mouths. "Everything is changing," Mulukan told them flatly. "If we don't move we will become like Antarctica, a place once warm and lush, but today frozen." Laughter tugged at the corners of her eyes. "A place that today is warming again." With a shake of her head, she added, "Everything is changing. What is hot today may very well be ice tomorrow. What is frozen today may be hot tomorrow. No one can stand still," she argued. "Yhwh will not allow it. We must change or perish. Our pain comes because we refuse to evolve."

The fighters, men who had sunk their culture and traditions deep into Onbil's soil, deeper than the Tropical Palm's roots went into the earth, remained deaf to Mulukan's words. They refused to hear her. Fear against change had produced a failing culture in Onbil.

Before Mulukan arrived, forests were being destroyed at a frightening and near suicidal rate. Only children of wealthy parents were allowed access to books and learning. With more than eighty percent of the island's population living on a meager thousand mescas a year, Mulukan knew what she had to do and she wasted no time getting to it. While she restored roadways, erected schools, revised Onbil's voting systems and tightened banking and other financial regulations, former leaders charged her with insolence, and screamed of uprising, but Mulukan held to the resolve she discovered years ago when she, a motherless child, set upon a lone hill in the plain that promised death with each breath, the spirit of her ancestors going over her skin with each passing breeze.

With Independence Day, Onbil's largest national celebration and the day in July 1950 when Onbil gained independence from Spain, only a day away, government offices, shops and rows of outdoor vending booths were decorated in purples, black, reds and yellows. Large trucks heavy with costumes, masks, face paint, log drums, arghul, a single reed woodwind instrument, and vahila, one of the most popular stringed instruments played in Onbil, lined the streets.

Tomorrow the instruments would be played by

talented musicians who would stand atop rosewood stage platforms, and, the musicians' lungs and fingers making the instruments alive, music would stream across much of the business district. Children took longer than usual to make their way home from school, opting to peek through the trucks' small, back windows or trek inside a local shop with friends, expectation and laughter stringing its way through the air that had somehow become light over the last several days.Mothers cooked chicken, fish curry, veal, rice and greens and lasopy, a fresh vegetable and meat bones soup, enough to feed ten families.

When their younger children inched their fingers over the kitchen table edge in the hopes of coming away with a chunk of the meal, the mothers, a chuckle tucked against their mouths, swatted at their child's small fingers and shouted, "Go play." Fathers, a long day of work at their backs, busied themselves nailing pieces of wood together. They didn't stop hammering the wood together until they stepped back and admired the small vending booth they'd recently constructed.

Independence Day was a time of great movement. Even the elder citizens could be seen at the edges of their homes plucking flowers from a garden or teasing their grandchildren so as to keep them out of their working parents' way. Everyone gave effort to clean Onbil. The flowers the elder citizens picked would be placed inside woven baskets and carried to the market on Independence Day, helping to explode colors across the land like a giant rainbow. Onbil became like a newborn during Independence Day. Each of her citizens wanted to care for her, draw closer to her and ensure she was growing strong.

Mulukan had been in office two full years. This was the first year she would attend Independence Day being that she was in the clinic this same time last year, a sniper's bullet having ruptured her thigh, lodging itself like fire beneath her hamstring. "I won't miss another one," she exclaimed to the Prime Minister the night she was rushed to a nearby clinic. She had been delivering a speech when gunshot erupted. Not yet a full paragraph into her address, she collapsed to the floor clutching her leg and stretched forth her hand to beckon for help.

On the eve of the present year's Independence Day, a fifty-year old holiday that had not been celebrated robustly in more than twenty years, just as the sun's rays began to turn away from Onbil, Mulukan looked out of her office window six floors up and watched squirrel, raccoon and lemur race across the dirt road, their feet scampering for the shade of trees. Alongside the hurrying animals, insects burrowed into the earth. Mulukan could not turn away from the heat. She was soon to walk directly into its fiery path. She had a speech to deliver.

Less than an hour later, she stood in the heat the animals and insects hurried away from. An army of security surrounded the stage she stood upon. The audience standing before her was made up of faces so numerous she could not count them. They appeared as numerous as pebbles at the ocean's edge. Hours ago they had left their homes in the villages to arrive at Market, Onbil's central business and government thoroughfare. Tomorrow, dancers, musicians, children, matriarchs and patriarchs would clamor here, their eyes bright, faces aglow with the celebrations of Independence Day. On this day, the eve of Independence Day, these people awaited what Mulukan would say, which direction she would tell them Onbil was destined to follow in the coming weeks and months, a course that would change and forever impact each of their lives.

Mulukan adjusted the microphone to the right height. She raised her shoulders until they looked like two sentries guarding her, keeping watch over her, holding up her ancestors and the people who gaped at her with collected curiosity.

Despite the high temperatures, not a drop of sweat dotted her forehead. Though the people standing before her were not from the community she was born into, were not the tribe her parents came from, Mulukan knew in her soul, at a level high above flesh and blood, that she had come home; she knew it.

A spirit of thanksgiving infused her speech. Dumpling clouds billowed across the sky. With one last adjustment to the microphone, Mulukan began, "Yhwh moving through us, our triumphs have been as rich, varied and numerous as we are. Onbil's education level has risen. Our national debt has been cut nearly in half, today at three hundred million, down from five hundred and fifty million, the point our debt was at two short years ago. We have a national health insurance program that has allowed all of Onbil's citizens access to medical treatment. No one living in Onbil has to suffer because they lack the means to pay for medical care.

We are a kindler, gentler Onbil. Our murder and theft rates have dropped. We are making progress. We are daring to change. Yet, I stand here before you today to tell you much work remains to be done and we are getting to it. There will always be work to do, as we live on an ever changing landscape, in a universe that never stills. We will cut loose from fear and evolve to greater and greater strength and deeper and deeper wisdom."

"Even as I speak we are working to create better export laws for Onbil. Next week I am traveling to meet with the leaders of A League of Nations. My stance remains unchanged. Onbil will remain relentless in its pursuit of stronger trade laws that allow Africa to have a fair playing field in the international markets. The importance of gaining these new trade laws may well be immeasurable. We need fair trade laws in order to compete with stronger, more dominant nations, and we will push until those new trade laws are signed into effect. Onbil's citizens and business owners will be allowed to barter and sell with the strongest businesses around the globe. We will gain access to the arenas that will allow us to earn economic wealth.

For those of you hoping for this, you are not alone. The entire Onbil government is fighting for you; we will gain victory. That is not all. We will continue to make safe our villages and educate to eradicate violence and crime. Two years from today, when I stand before you, it is my goal to have our national debt down to zero. I will give everything within my power and certainly trust in Yhwh to make that so. I am your servant, Onbil."

At once and as if the air had ceased to move, Mulukan's breath caught in her throat. She fastened her gaze upon a woman who looked to be buried amongst the sea of people, the color of their faces dark red and black, like the rosewood and ebony trees populating the island. The woman's long forehead, her broad nose, full mouth and dark, shining eyes transfixed Mulukan. Yet more than the woman's physical features it was the way the woman looked back at her that arrested Mulukan's attention. The woman looked at her as if she were as clear as the sky above, as if she could see through Mulukan's skin right to her heart. Their gazes locked and remained fastened upon one another for a long time.

Mulukan's voice deepened. She was almost shouting. "Guided by Yhwh, our going forward is with great promise. Former patterns will rise up and challenge us, but if you are truly ready to go forward, we will create a better Onbil for now, for generations to come." She gave the crowd a hard stare. "I need to know that you are ready to meet every challenge that threatens our great future. I need to know that you will join me and push through every wave of resistance, rolling strong and fierce like the tide in the Red Sea, which threatens to keep us locked to the past, days as dead as the garments Lazarus wore to the grave Christ called him away from."

At once Mulukan's hands shot into the air. "Then let us go now," she shouted. "Into our new, greater Onbil."

While the crowd roared, Mulukan fixed her gaze upon the woman, her hair bushy, her nose wide, her skin dark like ebony wood. Age lines crossing the woman's face made the woman look twice Mulukan's age, old enough to be her mother.

Mulukan's and the woman's gazes locked; they stood beneath the hot sun watching and probing each other until one of the eight security guards assigned to protect Mulukan crossed the stage and stepped into the mesmerizing scene. The guard tugged on Mulukan's arm. "We have to head back," the guard said. He didn't move until Mulukan turned away from staring at the woman and followed him.

That night, Mulukan drifted to sleep amid a nervous mental stir. The woman's face was lodged inside her mind, stuck there, as if the woman had been the only person, the only thing, Mulukan had seen in her entire life. Even with the comforts filling her bedroom, Mulukan was unable to go deep inside sleep's portal. On this night, her bedroom's expensive decorations, the flowery, beige fitted sheets, quilted bedspreads, four-poster treatments hung from a ceiling frame, multi-sized pillows, most of them large, the sofa, full bath, crystal vases filled with tall daisies, the three, large, gorgeous batik paintings, and the two short redwood tables, one upon which was placed a hand-crafted clock, offered no solace. This was unlike all the other nights she had entered her bedroom, and, despite the struggles that had come to her throughout the day, she had glanced about the room, and, looking at the decorations, had told herself she had come a long way. Then, being convinced the successes were hers, she had climbed into bed exhausted, yet satisfied, and had

fallen soundly asleep.

This night was different.

This night, outside Mulukan's bedroom, and as if somehow linked to the events from her childhood, the roads were quiet and empty. The roads stayed that way, the island seemingly resting, drinking up the hope that had spilled into the air, spilled like water dripping through a faucet, with each word Mulukan spoke during her speech earlier in the day.

Outside it stayed quiet until a bird, a pygmy kingfisher, flew onto one of the tallest branches of the tree whose branches shaded much of Mulukan's bedroom. Beneath the dispersing clouds, the pygmy kingfisher opened its long, pointy beak and started to sing.

While she slept, a deep breath filled Mulukan's lungs. The breath came out with a snort and a low-pitched rumble, sounds that stirred Mulukan away from sleep.

She rolled to her side and faced the window. It was then that she heard the bird's chirping.She lay still for several seconds, until an uneasy feeling came over her, a feeling that reminded her of something from the past. She stared across the room in bewilderment then she cleared her thoughts and sat up. "Odd time for a bird to be chirping," she said. Her gaze went across the room to the redwood table upon which sat the hand-crafted clock. "It's not even four in the morning."

She told herself to sink again beneath the covers, close her eyes and return to sleep. But she knew sleep would not come.

The room was dark with night. Stars stood in the sky like diamonds. The moon's glow spread across the island with a growing touch of light. And then Mulukan heard it, another pygmy kingfisher perched on the tree just outside her window, another pygmy kingfisher singing into the night.

Mulukan idled at the edge of the bed while fear coached her not to accept what could be. But a greater emotion, courage, pushed Mulukan up. She stood sluggishly and inched across the floor. Just as she reached out, her hand going to part the heavy drapes, she stopped.

A cool breeze went across the nape of her neck. The hair on her neck and arms rose and stiffened like straight pins. Her spine chilled at the thought that she was not alone.

She turned away from the window and the sound of the chirping pygmy kingfishers. Like an epilogue to her physical life's story, her mother stood in front of her with her arms extended, bidding Mulukan to come inside.

For the first time since the day back in the plain

when the community had painted their faces and danced and returned her mother's body to the earth, when Mulukan thought about and looked upon her mother, she wept. "I knew it was you," she said while she stared through the dark. She reached out for her mother. "I saw you in the crowd, your long forehead. Your soft smile. The way you wouldn't look away from me. I saw you, Mother." She took in a deep breath while she looked inside her mother's eyes. "You've been with me," she said. "You've been with me all along."

And for the rest of the night, the only sound Mulukan heard other than the sound of her own fast, falling tears, was the sound of the pygmy kingfishers chirping wildly outside her bedroom window.

"True love cannot be found where it truly doesn't exist, nor can it be hidden where it truly does."

African Proverb

Chapter Eight

Mulukan heard a knock at her office door and looked up. Her assistant, a mild mannered, stocky woman named Abayomi, was standing in the doorway. Because Abayomi was short, even while she was seated, Mulukan saw the man standing behind Abayomi.

As soon as Mulukan's gaze landed on the man's face, emotion surged through her body like electricity. Her hands started to shake, and her tongue felt thick in her mouth. She had only felt this way before once, and that had been over ten years ago when she interviewed for the communications writer position with President Abasi Nyathi. Mulukan remembered. She had felt this crush of emotion, this passion, spurn her toward the hope that she would one day fall in love, while Kokumuo guided her through art museums when she first arrived to Mariami.

Yet romance was not a sentiment Mulukan imagined herself to seek after. After years of being alone, she did not see life's lessons that taught her to see herself as a woman in love. Mulukan's focus was on empowering Africa. It was the visitations from her mother and other ancestors that made her know she was born in the earth to restore a part of Africa. In that she was not alone. There were witnesses to this truth. Mulukan saw the witnesses when she crossed paths with the man from the market, Desta back in the village, President Abasi Nyathi and Kokumuo. She saw witnesses when she attended inter-continental heads of nation meetings. Since she was a young girl, she had been prepared to give the total sum of her energy to care for and strengthen Africa.

Africa was her home. These were her people and she knew like all of Yhwh's creations, that they would return to the greatness from whence they sprang. All they had to do was to wake up and remember who they truly were not who they thought themselves to be. That day would come, Mulukan knew. Her efforts combined with the efforts of the other witnesses would hasten the arrival of that day. Its promise was tucked inside shared truths. Africa would remember; Africa would awaken to Yhwh.

But love presented as the face of romance, that Mulukan did not think to be a part of her life. She did not see romance as a thread that weaved its way through her earth experience. She did not gaze upon her physical reflection in mirrors or deep noisy waters and see a man longingly at her side. She but worked well with men. They were a part of the architecture of her working life. Men stayed on the surface of her experience. Men did not sink within her heart the way acacia tree seeds go into the belly of the earth then, after many days, push up and reveal their strength, their beauty, their joy, their sway -- their dance. How could they? The first man Mulukan loved returned to the earth when she was a child. It seemed people didn't remain in their bodies long enough to go like seeds deep inside Mulukan's heart. People in Mulukan's childhood were like seeds that blew across the ground, that were plucked up too soon. Baobab never grew fruit in Mulukan's life because the storms of her childhood uprooted the hope of romantic love before it had time to produce sweet fruit.

Mulukan grew hot. Emotions stirred within her then exploded into joy. The attachment she felt to Kokumuo came to her with a familiar song. In so many ways she had felt this way before. Yet, all those years ago she thought she was just nervous. She never thought she was in love. But she could not deny it now. She wondered how she missed it. She wondered how this truth slipped past her psyche while at the same time it had gone deep inside her heart.

Abayomi stepped to the side.

Kokumuo's thick frame filled the doorway.

"Mulukan, this is Kokumuo Kenyatta. He said you two worked together for President Nyathi back in Mariami." Abayomi nodded at Mulukan, then she turned and walked across the hall and back inside her own office. A second later, and although the long hallway provided Mulukan ample privacy, Abayomi closed her office door. There was something in Kokumuo's smile and Mulukan's eyes that told Aboyami she had witnessed the beginnings of a sacred contract shared between two people who were on a joint journey. Her father and mother had taught her to respect that pearl experience and so Aboyami closed her office door.

"Kokumuo," Mulukan said as she stood from her cherry oak desk. While she looked into Kokumuo's penetrating eyes she wondered if this had been what her mother came to tell her last night. That someone would come into her life and bathe her in the love she thought only her father and mother could bring to her. She wondered if her mother had spoke a brief farewell to her, an interlude, to allow her to make room inside her thoughts and inside her heart for Kokumuo's love. As a child, Mulukan had overheard her mother laugh to another woman back in the plain that, "Two trees can't stand in the same spot of ground, but a billion trees can share the earth."

Kokumuo was silent. In the silence, he admired Mulukan. Her face, though firm and set, seemed somehow softer than when he first appeared in the doorway. Her usually round and taut shoulders had risen and squared since he last saw her. Her eyes were clear. Her gaze was fixed.

She had met with success, Kokumuo knew. It showed in her body. It was painted across her face. The resilience Kokumuo saw in Mulukan twelve years ago when they worked together had served her well.

Kokumuo read the newspaper articles. He saw the stories blasted across television and computer screens. Mulukan had met with death threats. She had been shot while delivering one of her early public addresses. Yet, she had not cowered. She had not backed away from what Yhwh called her to. She stood in the 'between' with a passion that went deep and wide like rushing water. Mulukan stayed on course despite the winds that came to uproot her.

The longer Kokumuo looked at Mulukan the

more he realized he had never met a woman like Mulukan before.Mulukan's concern was for all of Africa's citizens. She was a mother to the continent, and she would not abandon those she loved. Kokumuo wondered how he missed it. Mulukan and he were on the same path. Their lives were entwined in their passions, in their purpose. For so long Kokumuo thought he had to journey earth's path alone, but now, while he looked inside Mulukan's eyes, he knew with a certainty that shook his bones, that from this day forward he would complete his earth journey coupled with Mulukan.

He had so much to tell Mulukan. They had never talked much about their families. Mulukan didn't know that Kokumuo was an orphan. When he was six years old, his parents were forced to the edge of their home, then lined up against their front door and shot in the head by rebel soldiers. Kokumuo crouched inside a wood box ten feet away. The guns blasted and blood spurted out of Kokumuo's parents' skulls like water coming out of a fountain. It landed on Kokumuo's feet and turned them red.

The shootings made Kokumuo like a lost boy gone from his tribe, gone from warmth in the world, at the peak of a brutal and bloody Congo war. It was as though Mulukan and he had no past. For Kokumuo that was as it should be. Although he was often judged against it, Kokumuo knew the past was full of unalterable events. Kokumuo knew the past was dead. Not even Yhwh changed the past. Not even Yhwh made it so that yesterday's rains didn't wet the earth. What had happened, had happened. It was his root that Kokumuo desired to share with Mulukan. He wanted to tell her he loved his father's loud, robust laughter and his father's compassion. He wanted to tell her how warm he felt each time his mother held him inside her arms while he sat in her lap. He wanted to tell her that he felt the way he imagined a bowl felt when it was poured full to the brim with hot, delicious soup. He wanted to tell Mulukan about the rare, lazy days he had spent at college when he was younger.

"Can you believe I came here on vacation?" Kokumuo asked.

Mulukan chuckled. Absent forethought, she rounded her desk and walked closer to Kokumuo.

"I came here with another woman." The words came out with haste. Kokumuo didn't realize their impact until he saw the open and aghast expression explode upon Mulukan's face. "No. No," he tried again while he raised his hands in effort to halt the spread of confusion and hurt dressing Mulukan's face. "That is really how I came to be here. That's really how it happened. I am being honest with you, but," he added with poignant tenderness, "I am not going to hurt you."

Mulukan leaned back and peered at Kokumuo. For a long time, he had perplexed her. While she listened to him talk, she realized she didn't know the inner details of his life. She didn't know about the experiences he'd had or the choices he'd made outside of work, experiences and choices that shaped him into the man he was today.

She admired Kokumuo. In truth, she adored him. She knew she could not fight it. She wanted to be with Kokumuo. And so rather than argue and scream, she walked to the front of her desk and leaned against the edge. "Go on," she offered with a gentle smile.

"It wasn't until we got here that I saw patterns in my lady friend I didn't like but chose to ignore so many times."

Mulukan kept silent. She didn't want to do or say anything to disrupt Kokumuo's thoughts. She wanted the details.

"I took her to the most popular spots on the island. It didn't matter. Wherever I took her, she found something wrong. When she found something wrong, I hurried and took her someplace else. I was trying so hard to make her happy. After two days of that, I gave up. The next time she complained, I told her I was going to go my way and she could go her way and that the two were not the same."

Kokumuo looked at the floor, then he quickly raised his head and gazed inside Mulukan's eyes. Her brow remained tight, but not as tight as it was when he first told her he had come to the island with another woman. He could tell Mulukan was listening to him. Her eyes darted and revealed that she was clinging to each word he spoke. That told him one thing; Mulukan loved him as much as he loved her. That truth danced emotion across his spine.

The truth that Mulukan loved him tugged at the corners of his mouth and turned his lips into a smile. "We parted ways yesterday. She returned to Mariami. And," he added with a twinkle in his eye, "I'm glad."

"So, you came here on vacation?"

"Yes."

"And nothing else?"

He moved close to Mulukan. "So, I thought."

"What?" Mulukan smiled. "Did you forget that I was leading this great nation?"

He returned her smile. "I didn't forget."

Silence passed between them, then Mulukan looked at Kokumuo and said, "I'm glad you're here, Kokumuo. I want you to be here."

"Needing a friend?" Before she answered, he asked, "Or is there not a special man in your life?" He paused. "I certainly hope it's the latter."

Mulukan crossed her arms. "You come over here with another woman and now you're telling me you hope I don't have a special man in my life?"

"Mulukan, are we blind?"

She uncrossed her arms and raised a brow.

"We've always known what we know right now."

Mulukan was silent.

"We've always loved each other," Kokumuo said.

"I don't think I ever thought of you in romantic terms."

Kokumuo laughed. "Of course not. We both

were too busy working to think of anything except work."

"True."

Kokumuo looked at the pen and paper trays on Mulukan's desk. He admired the long peach drapes hanging from the office windows. The cherry wood furniture gave off a crisp scent that was easy on his nose. Mulukan had achieved what he knew she would the day she stepped in and delivered the public address for President Nyathi after he took ill. He recalled the fear in Mulukan's eyes that day. She was angry with him for telling her she was going to give the speech. He knew she wanted him to address the crowd because she trusted his skills more than she trusted herself.

He also knew Mulukan had resolve. She was a woman with an open heart. Hers was an admirable will. He respected her balance. She wasn't too hard and she wasn't too soft. She was like a warm sweater that fit perfectly, that warmed his heart to perfection. She was the woman he had dreamed about since he was in school. She complimented him. They filled in weakened places in each other's lives. He didn't know why he didn't see it before. Mulukan and he were meant to be together.

"We've done well together, Mulukan."

"We have."

"Let's not stop that."

She smiled a toothy grin.

Kokumuo took a chance. He wanted Mulukan and his relationship to move forward and become what it was meant to be. "Mulukan, what do you feel while you look at me? What's going through your mind? What do you feel in your heart?"

Mulukan stared into the empty hallway.

"If you're afraid to tell me, why are you afraid?"

Mulukan remained silent.

"I'll go first," Kokumuo finally said. "I hope you'll share what you feel too." He swallowed. "I didn't realize it until now. I have always loved you,

Mulukan. I always knew you had greatness in you. It's your born nature I love. Whenever I'm with you, I feel warm. I feel love. The only other time I can remember feeling like I do when I'm with you is when I'm with my grandmother. I feel loved and perfect when I'm with you. I felt that way even during those times when it was clear I had gotten on your nerves." He laughed. "You appreciate, Mulukan. You're not a complainer. You focus on what you want. You're grateful for what comes your way." He shook his head. "I can't believe I'm standing here. I came here for a totally different reason. But I'm right where I should be. I'm with the woman I should be with for the rest of my earth life."

Emotion pooled in Mulukan's eyes. "What do I feel, Kokumuo? You want to know?" Tears she'd ached to shed while she roamed villages and streets alone as an orphan, moans she'd wished to release up to heaven after she received death threats, the longings she felt for affection as she slept alone at night as if only she, a woman amid millions of other women, could never be warmed with the certainly that she was wanted by a man - it all came together like a storm, then it erupted. It was like a flood of rain going up. It was like a volcano. The desire revealed itself so suddenly, Mulukan had not the time to rearrange what she meant to say, what her heart demanded to let go. The words rushed out. "I love you." She closed the distance that separated them. Like a cool breeze pushing up, she raised her arms and wrapped them around Kokumuo's back. She squeezed him tightly. They held on to each other for a long time. "I love you," Mulukan repeated while she rested her head on Kokumuo's shoulder.

Outside her office pygmy kingfishers perched on the tallest limbs of a tree. Luscious fruit swayed from the tree's branches like huge burnt orange diamonds. The birds' joyous song soared above the tree and filled the sky with music.

Read More Books by Denise Turney

Love Pour Over Me

Portia (Denise's 1st book)

Long Walk Up

Pathways To Tremendous Success

Rosetta The Talent Show Queen

Rosetta's Great Adventure

Design A Marvelous, Blessed Life

Spiral

Love Has Many Faces

Your Amazing Life

Awaken Blessings of Inner Love

Book Marketing That Drives Up Book Sales

Love As A Way Of Life

It Starts with Love

Love The Journey

Gada's Glory

Escaping Toward Freedom (new book)

Visit Denise Turney online

www.chistell.com

Made in the USA
Las Vegas, NV
23 June 2023

73794992ROO066